Adelia Cleopatra Graves

Jephthah's Daughter

A Drama in Five Acts

Adelia Cleopatra Graves

Jephthah's Daughter
A Drama in Five Acts

ISBN/EAN: 9783337342456

Printed in Europe, USA, Canada, Australia, Japan

Cover: Foto ©Andreas Hilbeck / pixelio.de

More available books at **www.hansebooks.com**

Jephthah's Daughter.

A Drama in Five Acts,

Founded on the Eleventh Chapter of Judges.

By Mrs. Adelia C. Graves,

*Professor of Rhetoric and former Professor of Latin and Belles-Lettres,
in Mary Sharp College, Winchester, Tenn.*

Memphis, Tenn,:
SOUTH-WESTERN PUBLISHING HOUSE.
1867.

To the Pupils

OF THE

Mary Sharp College,

*With whom I have spent many of the pleasantest
hours of my life,*

This Little Work

Is most affectionately inscribed.

*May they be stimulated to all
deeds worthy of Woman; then will each be
worthy of self and her*

Alma Mater.

PREFACE.

FROM my earliest girlhood, the history of Jephthah's Daughter, told as it is in so few words, and yet those few beautifully revealing to us a character perfect in its simplicity, and uniting, without the slightest ostentation, every element of feminine excellence, has had a peculiar charm for me.

The coolest courage, the most undaunted heroism, the loftiest patriotism, consummated in the extremest act of self-sacrifice humanity can perform, were all present in her ready concurrence in her father's dreadful vow; and yet the simple Israelitish maiden seems to have thought only of filial obedience and right.

And the stern majesty of Jephthah, outcast and insulted; feeling keenly the wrongs he suffered, yet, by his determination and energy, aided by the blessing of the God he served, patiently working out a reputation which finally triumphed, and brought him the honor for which he toiled so long and faithfully, has been a favorite subject for study.

The master-passion of his nature I have made pride; fostered by the unfortunate circumstances of his life, and which, from his feeling his own worthiness, made him esteem himself just in proportion to the disesteem, or contempt of others; and which, so long as it led only to a just appreciation of himself, was right; but in excess became a wrong, as spoken by Telah, in scene first:

> What was
> Humility and faith at first,
> May grow into self-confidence
> And pride; and right, pursued too far
> Or with unholy motive, grow
> Into a wrong,—

inculcating the doctrine that all vices are but excesses of some virtue.

If I have preserved the unity of my plot and exhibited the character of Jephthah throughout, as it naturally would exhibit itself under the influence of this predominant passion, I have accomplished all I expected.

MARY SHARP COLLEGE,
   WINCHESTER, TENN.,
      May 1, 1867.

HISTORY.

AND after Abimelech there arose to defend Israel, Tola, the son of Puah, the son of Dodo, a man of Issachar; and he dwelt in Shamir in mount Ephraim. And he judged Israel twenty and three years, and died, and was buried in Shamir.

And after him arose Jair, a Gileadite, and judged Israel twenty and two years. And he had thirty sons that rode on thirty ass colts, and they had thirty cities, which are called Havoth-jair unto this

day, which are in the land of Gilead.
And Jair died, and was buried in Camon.
And the children of Israel did evil again
in the sight of the Lord, and served
Baalim, and Ashtaroth, and the gods of
Syria, and the gods of Zidon, and the
gods of Moab, and the gods of the chil-
dren of Ammon, and the gods of the
Philistines, and forsook the Lord, and
served not him.

And the anger of the Lord was hot
against Israel, and he sold them into the
hands of the Philistines, and into the
hands of the children of Ammon. And
that year they vexed and oppressed the
children of Israel eighteen years, all the
children of Israel that were on the other
side Jordan in the land of the Amorites,
which is in Gilead. Moreover, the chil-

dren of Ammon passed over Jordan, to fight also against Judah, and against Benjamin, and against the house of Ephraim; so that Israel was sore distressed.

And the children of Israel cried unto the Lord, saying, We have sinned against thee, both because we have forsaken our God, and also served Baalim. And the Lord said unto the children of Israel, Did not I deliver you from the Egyptians, and from the Amorites, from the children of Ammon, and from the Philistines? The Zidonians also, and the Amalekites, and the Maonites, did oppress you; and ye cried to me, and I delivered you out of their hand. Yet ye have forsaken me, and served other gods: wherefore I will deliver you no more. Go and cry unto the gods which ye have chosen; let them deliver you in the time of your tribulation.

And the children of Israel said unto the Lord, We have sinned: do thou unto us whatsoever seemeth good unto thee; deliver us only, we pray thee, this day. And they put away the strange gods from among them, and served the Lord: and his soul was grieved for the misery of Israel. Then the children of Ammon were gathered together, and encamped in Gilead. And the children of Israel assembled themselves together, and encamped in Mizpeh. And the people and princes of Gilead said one to another, What man is he that will begin to fight against the children of Ammon? he shall be head over all the inhabitants of Gilead.

Now Jephthah the Gileadite was a mighty man of valor, and he was the son of a harlot: and Gilead begat Jephthah. And Gilead's wife bare him sons; and his wife's sons grew up, and they thrust out Jephthah, and said unto him, Thou shalt not inherit in our father's house; for thou art the son of a strange woman. Then Jephthah fled from his brethren, and dwelt in the land of Tob: and there were gathered vain men to Jephthah, and went out with him.

And it came to pass in process of time, that the children of Ammon made war against Israel. And it was so, that when the children of Ammon made war against Israel, the elders of Gilead went to fetch Jephthah out of the land of Tob: And they said unto Jephthah, Come, and be our captain, that we may fight with the children of Ammon. And Jephthah said unto the elders of Gilead, Did not ye hate me, and expel me out of my father's house? and why are ye come unto me now when ye are in distress? And the elders of Gilead said unto Jephthah, Therefore we turn again to thee now, that thou mayest go with us, and fight against the children of Ammon, and be our head over all the inhabitants of Gilead. And Jephthah said unto the elders of Gilead, If ye bring me home again to fight against the children of Ammon, and the Lord deliver them before me, shall I be your head? And the elders of Gilead said unto Jephthah, The Lord be a witness between us, if we do not so according to thy words.

Then Jephthah went with the elders of Gilead, and the people made him head and captain over them: and Jephthah uttered all his words before the Lord in Mizpeh.

And Jephthah sent messengers unto the king of the children of Ammon, saying, What hast thou to do with me, that thou art come against me to fight in my land? And the king of the children of Ammon answered unto the messengers of Jephthah, Because Israel took away my land, when they came up out of Egypt, from Arnon even unto Jabbok, and unto Jordan: now therefore restore those lands again peaceably. And Jephthah sent messengers again unto the king of the children of Ammon; and said unto him, Thus saith

Jephthah, Israel took not away the land of Moab, nor the land of the children of Ammon: but when Israel came up from Egypt, and walked through the wilderness unto the Red Sea, and came to Kadesh; then Israel sent messengers unto the king of Edom, saying, Let me, I pray thee, pass through thy land: but the king of Edom would not hearken thereto. And in like manner they sent unto the king of Moab; but he would not consent. And Israel abode in Kadesh. Then they went along through the wilderness, and compassed the land of Edom, and the land of Moab, and came by the east side of the land of Moab, and pitched on the other side of Arnon, but came not within the border of Moab: for Arnon was the border of

Moab. And Israel sent messengers unto
Sihon, king of the Amorites, the king
of Heshbon; and Israel said unto him,
Let us pass, we pray thee, through thy
land unto my place. But Sihon trusted
not Israel to pass through his coast: but
Sihon gathered all his people together,
and pitched in Jahaz, and fought against
Israel. And the Lord God of Israel
delivered Sihon and all his people into
the hand of Israel, and they smote them:
so Israel possessed all the land of the
Amorites, the inhabitants of that country. And they possessed all the coasts
of the Amorites, from Arnon even unto
Jabbok, and from the wilderness even
unto Jordan. So now the Lord God
of Israel hath dispossessed the Amorites
from before his people Israel, and

2

shouldest thou possess it? Wilt not
thou possess that which Chemosh thy
god giveth thee to possess? So whom-
soever the Lord our God shall drive out
from before us, them will we possess.
And now art thou any thing better than
Balak, the son of Zippor, king of Moab?
did he ever strive against Israel, or did
he ever fight against them, while Israel
dwelt in Heshbon and her towns, and
in Aroer and her towns, and in all the
cities that be along by the coasts of
Arnon, three hundred years? why therefore did ye not recover them within that
time? Wherefore I have not sinned
against thee, but thou doest me wrong
to war against me: the Lord the Judge
be judge this day between the children
of Israel and the children of Ammon.

Howbeit the king of the children of Ammon hearkened not unto the words of Jephthah which he sent him.

Then the Spirit of the Lord came upon Jephthah, and he passed over Gilead, and Manasseh, and passed over Mizpeh of Gilead, and from Mizpeh of Gilead he passed over unto the children of Ammon. And Jephthah vowed a vow unto the Lord, and said, If thou shalt without fail deliver the children of Ammon into my hands, then it shall be, that whatsoever cometh forth of the doors of my house to meet me, when I return in peace from the children of Ammon, shall surely be the Lord's, and I will offer it up for a burnt-offering.

So Jephthah passed over unto the children of Ammon to fight against

them; and the Lord delivered them
into his hands. And he smote them
from Aroer even till thou come to Minnith, even twenty cities, and unto the
plain of the vineyards, with a very great
slaughter. Thus the children of Ammon were subdued before the children
of Israel.

And Jephthah came to Mizpeh unto
his house, and behold, his daughter came
out to meet him with timbrels and with
dances: and she was his only child;
besides her he had neither son nor
daughter. And it came to pass, when
he saw her, that he rent his clothes, and
said, Alas, my daughter! thou hast
brought me very low, and thou art one
of them that trouble me: for I have
opened my mouth unto the Lord, and I

can not go back. And she said unto him, My father, if thou hast opened thy mouth unto the Lord, do to me according to that which hath proceeded out of thy mouth; forasmuch as the Lord hath taken vengeance for thee of thine enemies, even of the children of Ammon. And she said unto her father, Let this thing be done for me: let me alone two months, that I may go up and down upon the mountains, and bewail my virginity, I and my fellows. And he said, Go. And he sent her away for two months: and she went with her companions, and bewailed her virginity upon the mountains. And it came to pass at the end of two months, that she returned unto her father, who did with her according to his vow which he had vowed: and she knew no man. And it was a custom in Israel, that the daughters of Israel went yearly to lament the daughter of Jephthah the Gileadite four days in a year.

CHARACTERS IN JEPHTHAH'S DAUGHTER.

JEPHTHAH—*The Gileadite.*

TELAH—*His wife.*

ADAH—*His daughter.*

EBER—*Betrothed of Adah.*

MICAH—*First captain of the guard.*

HEZRON—*Officer in charge of sick and wounded.*

MIRIAM—*Servant maid.*

Men of Gilead.
Followers of Jephthah.
Musicians, attendants, and chorus of young girls, in scene fifth.

JEPHTHAH'S DAUGHTER.

Scene First.

*Time, morning—a room in Jephthah's house in Miz-
peh—Jephthah and Telah alone.*

TELAH.

GOEST thou forth upon the hills
To-day? I would thou stayed'st at home.
Rumors there are of yet a war
With Ammon and the Israelites,
And much I fear some danger may
Beset the path thou tread'st. These deeds
Of violence, and blood, and strife,
Suit not a woman's heart. Jephthah,
Stay here, I shall be happier.

3   (25)

JEPHTHAH.

'Tis ever thus with all thy sex,
When glory beckons onward, then
Would they, timid and shrinking, fain
Forego the honor, for the fear.

TELAH.

Nay, Jephthah, nay, not so; at least,
Not altogether so. Thou know'st
In times of danger, woman may,
Nerved by her love for those most dear,
Be cool, and prompt, and ready, and
Unflinching as a man; her mind
As firm as his; her courage strong,
And deathless even. But is't not this?
Blood-glory hath no lure to tempt
A woman's heart. In *that*, she sees
Not the best good to those she loves,
Nor yet the human race. Thus hath
It been from the beginning, even;

Woman opposed to violence
And blood. *Man slays* and *woman
mourns.*
I'd fain persuade thee, Jephthah, from
This life of danger, toil and fear,
To quieter pursuits.

JEPHTHAH.

I do
Not bid thee, Telah, call thy maids,
And to thy loom and distaff, and
Thy 'broidery frames, as many a man
Might do.   Attentively, I list
To all thou say'st, for pleasant is
Thy counsel ever unto me,
And all thy words of interest
Are sweet.   Much do I owe to thee,
In that I've brought thee from thy friends,
And country, and thy kin, to this

Strange desert land, and linked so close
Thy tender lovingness to my
Rough ways. Too much of my lone life
Thou'st cheered for me to turn away,
Unheeding aught that thou would'st say.
Fear not this strife of Ammon and
The Israelites. I have no part
In it. 'Tis true that Ammon hath
Encroached still farther now. His host
Hath camped in Gilead; so 'tis said,
In Mizpeh's streets—a rumor brought
The tidings yester-even—and yet
Thou know'st, that tho' my brethren and
All kindred of my tribe dwell there,
I have no part among them, and
Their quarrel is not *mine.* Yet tho'
Cast out, an alien from my tribe,
Can we not be as happy here,
As if *we* dwelt in Gilead? Thou

And our sweet child, our Adah, dark-
Eyed dove, are treasures quite enough
For me, joined with the favor of
Jehovah.   He hath prospered me,
And all to which I've put my hands,
And spread my name abroad. 'Tis proof
That He, whom I have served, hath work
For me to do.   'Twas thus of old
He prospered those *He* set apart
For great and worthy deeds. *Thou* dost
Not shrink from duty, Telah, nor
Would have *me* turn my back, when *He*
Appoints the way?

TELAH.

            Thou needest not
To ask—and yet, I *would* we dwelt
At peace with Gilead and thy kin.
If they but knew thee as thou art,

They would admire and love, instead
Of hating, and would bring thee home
Again.   My heart *is* sad whene'er
I think of this estrangement, for
A woman's nature yearns for love,
And kindness from all those whom blood
And duty make akin to her.
So much, too, it affecteth *thee*, I grieve,
For it hath warped thy mind, I fear
Ofttimes, and made thee jealous, and
Suspicious of thy kind: caused thee
To set too high an estimate
Upon men's thoughts of thee. What *was*
Humility and faith, at first,
May grow into *self*-confidence
And *pride;* and right, pursued too far,
Or with unholy motive, grow
Into a wrong.   That thus it *is*
With thee, I know not; yet sometimes

I fear.   *There is no sin*, thou know'st,
Jehovah winketh at, and least
In those, by whom he manifests
His power.   Jephthah, turn not away.
Wrong, in exalted privilege,
With signal punishment, our God
Hath ever visited.

JEPHTHAH.

Thou read'st
My secret thoughts, and canst not much
Esteem him whom thou hast divined
So well.

TELAH.

Because I *do* esteem
So much—because I think *so well*
Of Jephthah—that my fine gold is
So pure, is why I'd have no *breath*
Of *taint* upon it, and no *speck*

Of *rust corrode.*
'T is why I tell him all my mind,
How that I fear, sometimes, it may
Be needlessly, his mind is warped;
Jehovah's favor is not all
His heart desires; that he, too much,
Cares for his fellow-men's esteem,
And the world's honor.   'T is because
I love, I fear.   Love, as thou know'st
Is anxious; hath a watchful heart,
A vigilant eye, and, for the loved
One, feels a coming evil, oft,
Ere it arrives.

(Enter an attendant, announcing guests.)

ATTENDANT.

Some Gileadites are come, who crave
An audience of Jephthah.   Shall
I bring them here?

Interview with Jephthah.

JEPHTHAH.

Aye, bring them here.

TELAH.

I will retire. *(She goes.)*

JEPHTHAH. *(Aside.)*

What can they want
Of Jephthah? All these many years,
Have I dwelt here unsought, uncared
For, and despised. Why seek me now?

(Enter Gileadites.)

Why come ye, men of Gilead,
This day, to me? Do ye not know
That Jephthah hath no part among
His father's sons? What errand is't
That brings ye here?

GILEADITES.

We come to tell
Thee of our sore distress. Thou know'st

3

How all the tribes of Israel, for
These many years, have suffered: how
Jair, the Gileadite, was Judge,
And, dying, slept in Camon: how
'Th' Israelites turned to strange gods,
Ashtaroth, and Baalim, and
The gods of Zidon, and the gods
Of Syria, of Moab, and
The Philistines, and of the sons
Of Ammon, too, and did forsake
Jehovah, and no longer serve
Him.   Then his anger wax-ed hot
Against his people, and he sold
Them into the Philistines' hands
For eighteen years—all Israel that
Was in the land of Gilead and
The Amorite.   And now they've crossed
The Jordan—those bold Ammonites
To take *their* lands from Judah, and

From Benjamin, and from the house
Of Ephraim.　*We are sore distressed.*

JEPHTHAH.

It is an ancient crime, to turn
Away from worshiping the true
And living God, and to bow down
To idols.　Ye know that, all their days,
Hath Israel done this thing, since first
The golden calf was made within
The wilderness of Sin, and all
The people bowed them down to it.
Grievous it is, and grievously
The Lord hath ever punished it.

GILEADITES.

We know: we know Israel *hath* sinned;
But now unto Jehovah, God,
We've turned, confessing we have sinned,

In that we've turned away from Him,
And served Baalim.

JEPHTHAH.

        And He bade
Ye call upon the gods, whom ye
Have chosen, to deliver you!
'T was just.

GILEADITES.

And then we cried again, and turned
Away from heathen gods, and with
Clean hearts did serve the Lord, and we
Besought him He would do what seemed
Him good, but to deliver us from
Our enemy, but this one time.
And now we know He pitieth
The wretchedness of Israel.
The Ammonitish host, e'en now,
A multitude, are gathered and

Encamped in Gilead, and we
Th' Israelites, assembled are,
Scarce twenty bow-shots from thy home
In Mizpeh.

JEPHTHAH.

Why are ye come here,
To tell these things to me? Long have
I known what hath befallen them—
Israel and Gilead. What is't
To me? Ye know I have no part
In Gilead. My brethren drove
Me out, and said, "Thou shalt have no
Inheritance with us." They could
Not take Jehovah's favor, else
Would they have *that* deprived me of.
But He hath prospered me and I
Have tried to serve Him. Valiant men
Have gathered to me, and the tribes

GILEADITES.

Therefore*–thou sayest–it is
Because we wronged thee, and did do
That very thing. Therefore we turn
Again to thee, and pray thee to
Go with us and to fight the hosts
Of Ammon; then to take thy place
In Gilead's house, and be our head
Over all the men of Gilead.
Thou wilt not, Jephthah, be more just
Than God? we turned to *Him* and *He*
Hath pitied us.

JEPHTHAH.

And if ye bring
Me home again, to fight for you,

---

* It would seem not unlikely, from the reply of
the men of Gilead to Jephthah's question, and the
manner of his asking it, that some of his brethren
were among them.—JUDGES XI: 7, 8.

Against the hosts of Ammon, and
If God, through me, deliver ye
From out their hand, surely shall I
Then be your head in Gilead?

GILEADITES.

God be a witness between thee
And us, if we do not, even
According to thy words.

JEPHTHAH.

Then will
I send my messengers, this day
Unto th' Ammonitish king,
Saying, "And what hast thou to do
With me, that thou art come against
Me now, to take away my land?
When Israel wandering, came up out
Of Egypt through the desert, then
They asked of Sihon, king of all

The Amorites, saying, 'Let us pass,
We pray thee, through thy land unto
Our place.'   But he then gathered up
His men, and fought all Israel, and
The God of Israel gave Sihon
And all his people unto *them*,
The host of his own Israelites.
So they possessed the lands of all
Those Amorites, from Arnon even
Unto Jabbok's hill, and to the flood
Of Jordan, from the wilderness.
Take *thou* the land which Chemosh, *thine
Own god*, hath given *thee* to possess,
And thus will *we* possess even whom
The *Lord, our God*, shall drive out from
Before *our* face.   While Israel dwelt
In Heshbon, and her towns, and in
Aroer and her villages,
And in the cities, which grew up

Along the shores of Arnon for
Three hundred years, why did ye not
Recover them in all that time?
I have not trespassed thus on thee.
Thou doest wrong to war against
Me now. The Lord, the Judge, BE *Judge*
This day between the children of
His Israel and the Ammonites."
Thus will I say to him, and send
This day by some sure messenger.
Then, peradventure, if the Lord
Deliver Israel by my hand,
I shall be head in Gilead.
I'll be with ye anon.   *(Exit Gileadites.)*

(Soliloquizing.) There's a
Strong tie in blood. Affection may
Be warm, and true, e'en unto death,
But the affinity of blood

Is something different. Friendship
   speaks
Sentiments of variance
With zeal, and warmth, and earnestness,
And blame, but is not friendship as
Before. The bond will break, and what
Remains is hollow mockery
Of seeming only, and no more.
Friendship mounts guard; observes the
   rules,
The courtesies, civilities
Conventionalities of life,
But blood hath confidence in the
Born tie that holds together all,
And can dispense with forms.
Friendship *asks* favors; blood *demands*,
And feels it hath a right. Friendship
Aggrieved, can scarce converse about
A wrong, but weightier grows th' offense,

And wider is the breach than 'twas
At first; and confidence again
Returneth, never as before.
'Tis not in nature thus to be.
But blood grows hot and leaps its bounds,
And says hard words, and doeth wrong,
E'en grievous wrong, but when the heat
Of anger cools, and sorrow comes
To him who said the words, and did
The wrong, blood helpeth to forget,
And to forget is to forgive.
I know not yet, if *I* forgive;
I know I've not forgotten, for
The sting is here of all the taunts,
And scorn, and wrong of earlier years.
Yet sweet the triumph of the hour,
And sweeter 'twill be, when I am
Deliverer of Israel,
And head of Gilead.   I feel

The power struggling within me, and
My confidence unshaken that
Jehovah's might will manifest
Itself in me, and Ammon shall
Be driven from all the lands he hath
Usurped. Hear me, O! Lord, thou God
Of Israel, if, without fail,
Thou shalt deliver to my hands
The hosts of Ammon, then it shall
Be, that whatever cometh forth
From out the doors of mine own house
To meet me, when, victorious, I
Return in peace, a conqueror of
The Ammonites, shall surely be
The Lord's, and *I will offer it*
To Him for a burnt-offering.

ᴇɴᴅ ᴏꜰ ꜱᴄᴇɴᴇ ꜰɪʀꜱᴛ.

Scene Second.

Jephthah sitting in the door of his tent, after the Ammonites are subdued, his face buried in his hands.

JEPHTHAH.

(He rises and walks, soliloquizing.)

'Tis over now, the victory is fairly won;
Victory, to me, in senses more than one.
Jehovah nerved this arm.   An Ammon-
    ite
No vantage hath to fight an Israelite.
Baal-berith's   strength,   Baal-berith's
    mighty power,
Fail, ere the cloud-drops dry upon the
    flower,

And scattered thousands, on the blood-
    stained earth,
Embrace the soil that gave them first
    their birth.
E'en twenty cities more are Israel's own,
And through them Jephthah's name is
    proudly known;
That name once hated and cast out of
    men,
Who now entreat e'en Jephthah back
    again.
Oh! for this hour have 1 toiled and
    prayed,
And offerings on Jehovah's altar laid.
This hour, in fancy, have I thought so
    sweet,
None other could at all compare with it;
The crowning moment of dull strug-
    gling years,

Battle Scene.

The hope made certain from the depth
    of fears.
'T is come at last, tho' tardily. No more
An outcast, I may seek my father's door,
Enter and be his child again; yea, claim
My birthright, as the eldest of his name.
Thanks to Jehovah! praise and glory be
To Him who gave such joyful victory.

(Enter Eber.)

EBER.

Methought I heard thy signal calling me,
My leader's summons should not be in
    vain.

JEPHTHAH.

I did not call, yet art thou welcome
    here.
Is all prepared for our departure, when
The sun is risen in the east?

4

EBER.

All is prepared.

JEPHTHAH.

I am impatient now the conflict 's past.
Aroer, Minnith, and the towns between,
E'en twenty cities of the Ammonites,
Subdued, the country wrested from the
    foe,
The plain of vineyards bounds our con-
    quests now,
And Ammon Israel need no longer fear.
All 's done which I have come to do,
    and now
The land of Tob recalls my panting
    breast,
And weary limbs to rest them there,
    awhile,   [smile
And two sweet faces I would fain see

In loving fondness as I come again.
Thou 'rt ready, Eber?

EBER.

Ready! yes, my sire.
Pardon my boldness that I dare recall
Thy promise of the bliss that should be
    mine
When this foray was over, won by
    thee.
Surely thou canst not think I'd linger
    here!
My thoughts will far outstrip the stately
    march
My feet must keep among thy cooler
    hosts
That have no promised bride to greet,
When Mizpeh opens to their coming
    sight.

I would we went to-night, and need
    not wait
The op'ning day.

JEPHTHAH.

        Ah! youth is ever thus,
Impatient of a short delay. It is a stern,
Hard lesson, man must learn, to bide
    his time,
Nor strive to hasten what betideth him.
'Twill come, at last, be't good or ill,
    and thou
Wilt find many events thou'dst fain
    delay;
While there are others, that we wait so
    long,
So anxiously, and with such feverish
    thought   [while
Boding, and brooding; hoping, fearing,

The heart, sick with its own impatience,
 feeds
Upon itself, and eats its own core out,
Ere the desire's accomplished. Such,
 have I
Felt in the long and dreary years gone
 by,
My son—for gladly shall I call thee so,
I have none other; thou and she are all—
These heart-sick feelings may'st thou
 never know;
Nor canst thou, for thy lot will not be
 mine,
Brave, cherished scion of a noble line.

EBER.

Pardon my far presuming, if I ask
Hath Jephthah's name not been an
 honored one,

Famed, among Gilead's hills, for valor
 and
Such wisdom as a leader well becomes?
Did not men gather to his standard, and
Did he not then instruct, reform and
 prove,
Not leader only, but their benefactor,
 too?
Taming their fierce hearts to a calm
 control,
Making them better, happier than be-
 fore?
Hath not the poor blessed Jephthah, as
 he passed,
And orphans' tears, and widows' grate-
 ful prayers,
Have they not, too, been offered up for
 thee?
And now, to thine inheritance restored,

Leader of Gilead's submissive hosts,
Thou, sure, art satisfied!

JEPHTHAH.

                    Yea, satisfied.
It is for this I 've toiled and planned so
    long,
E'en from that hour of causeless wrong,
    when they
Did say to Jephthah, in his father's house,
And he, that father, said not one faint
    "Nay,"
"Begone!"   *   *   *   *
My heart hath nourished, in its secret
    core,
Those taunting words, those gestures of
    contempt,
Those haughty looks, when bent their
    brows on me,

In bitter, biting scorn.   Thou know'st
    not what
It is to feel one's self derided, mocked,
Jeered at with insult, hatred, foulest
        wrong;
To bear gibes, sneers, and looks askant,
        that say
"Thou 'rt made of meaner, dirtier clay
        than we;"
While he that should protect thee with
        an arm
Of power, stands silently and coldly by,
And not a glance of kindness warms his
        eye.
I hate the memory of those torturing
        years,
When oft with wild desire yet feeble hope
I sought for kindly offices, yea, menial
        ones,

E'en abject servitude, if by it I might
   gain
But one approving glance, humbling
   myself
E'en to the very dust, and yet repelled
As some loathed and degraded object,
   when
My soul was full of lofty thoughts, and
   full
And free forgiveness, melting love and
   joy
In my great, overmastering desire
To be beloved; or less, kindly endured.
O! Eber, I have borne all this, and
   more;
And, in stern silence, nursed such bitter
   wrongs
As would have made me desperate,
   wert not

For those most precious ones, my wife
    and child;
And for the confidence *my time would*
    come.
'Tis not what men may say of us that
    makes
Us vile: 'tis what we do.   The wrong
    must be
Within ourselves; lives out of sight oft-
    times,
And like the fruit of Sodom's apple, fair
And good to outward view, the foul,
    black heart
Hath but the dust and ashes of deceit
Within.

(Enter Micah, first Captain of the Guard, with a
    respectful salute to Jephthah.)

MICAH.

What disposition wilt thou that we make

Of all the prisoners to-night? Our band
Is small, thou know'st.

JEPHTHAH.

      See to 't they be secure.
Let a strict watch be set of one in ten;
Fewer might be unsafe: and let none
    sleep
Upon his post. Our band *is* small, be
    sure,
Some less than when we left our homes,
    and yet
Fewer are gone than we might have
    supposed,
Thanks to the justice of our cause and
    that
Great Power that hath protected us.
    They 're safe—
Our hostages, the chief men of the foe—

The Ammonites? They must be guard-
    ed with
Untiring vigilance.

MICAH.

                    Enough, my lord,
'T is Kadesh hath the charge of them,
    and he
Will not a whit abate his constant care.
A desert lion is he to his prey, and none
Shall plunder it from him.   Escape
Is scarcely possible, when he hath charge.
His fierce eye never seems in need of
    sleep.

JEPHTHAH.

'T is well; I know none I could better
    trust.
                    (*Turns away.*)

EBER. *(To Micah.)*

Say, Micah, wilt not thou rejoice, when
     this
One night is over in this bloody land,
And we turn homeward to the quiet
     shade,
And pleasant rest of Mizpeh's sheltering
     walls?

MICAH.

Why, lad, art not afraid to tarry here?
Thou did'st use gloriously the bow and
     spear,
And, for so young a lad, dost promise
     well;   [come?
Yet blenchest thou because the dark has

EBER.

Out on thee, Micah!   Nay, ten thousand
     nays.

Blanches my cheek nor at the dark, nor
    blood,
Though thou dost taunt me with my
    youth
And fear, a thing unknown to me. Thy
    age
Protects thee, else should'st thou repent
    thy taunts.
Surely there is no wrong that I'll rejoice
To tread once more in Mizpeh's streets.
    My home
Is there. *(Turns and walks indignantly away.)*

JEPHTHAH.

Nay, Eber, curb thy heart of fire:
Remain.

MICAH. *(Aside.)*

A hot head truly!   I had best take care.
(Aloud to Jephthah.)

What preparations for the morning shall
    we make?

JEPHTHAH.

      None, save to start at rising sun.
Let a picked company of archers lead
The way.   Next, march the prisoners,
    two and two,
And spearmen close behind.   The
    wounded then,
In litters take the way, while all the
    rear
Shall covered and protected be, of right,
By the most trusty of my veteran band.

MICAH.

Thou art determined that our pris'ners
    keep
Their lives secure?—the Ammonitish
    king

And his chief men, by whose advice he
    brought
This war on Israel?   Is 't well, my lord?
Our fathers did not so.   The heathen
    they
Spared not, but slew them, small and
    great.

JEPHTHAH.

Micah, thou dost forget thyself, yet for
Past services, I overlook thy forward-
    ness.
Thou art a veteran, brave and trusty,
    too,
And so I tell thee that we war not with
A fallen foe to practice cruelty.
These hostages are better for the peace
Of Gilead than if all their necks were
    merged

In one, and severed at a blow. Know'st
     not
That mercy, oftentimes, availeth more
Than strict, nay, even just severity?
We have not fought as Joshua, at God's
Command, to drive the heathen from
     the land,
But to repel encroachment, and when
     they
Who did the thing, submit, it is enough.

MICAH.

Thou dost command our forces by the
     way?

JEPHTHAH.

Even so: I lead our brave victorious
     band
To Mizpeh's gates, and there dismiss
     them to
5

Their homes.   But the picked guard I
    leave to march
With the poor sufferers in this bloody
    fray,
And our illustrious prisoners will be
Commanded by this noble youth. *(Aside.)*
    'Tis time
He try his powers, if he be worthy of
    the prize
I've promised him. *(To Eber.)* Eber, upon
    the way
See thou the Ammonitish king, and all,
Be treated generously, and yet take care
He be most strictly watched in word
    and deed.

EBER.

I fear thy captains will not like to be
Subjected to my orders. One so young

Hath not enough experience to be
Thus trusted, thus exalted over all
The brave, tried followers of thy veteran
    band.
Wilt please thee, name some other one?

MICAH. *(Aside.)*

                       Beshrew
Me, but the lad has sense. If 'twere
    not for
Such modest airs no step of mine should
    stir,   [dawn.
To do his bidding, at the morrow's

JEPHTHAH.

Eber, I will thou take the lead. I'll
    have
No other one. Look to it, Micah, that
All yield obedience to him as if
It were myself. Dost hear?

MICAH.

Dost think
Me deaf?   I hear as well as any one.
I know my duty, too, and shall not fail
To do it.

EBER.

Micah, thou hear'st what
Jephthah says: [struct
Thou must be privy counsellor, and in-
Me as to all that I must say and do.
Then 'twill be well: I have great con-
fidence
In thee.

MICAH.

I'll do it, lad. Thy judg-
ment's good. *(Aside.)*
I'm quite content. *(To Jephthah.)* Hast any
more commands?

JEPHTHAH.

Send Hezron here. *(Exit Micah; enter Hezron.)*
(To Hezron.) The wounded, how
are they?

HEZRON

Some better, and some worse.

JEPHTHAH.

The litters, for
To-morrow's use,—are they all ready
now?

HEZRON

All are made ready, or will be before
We sleep.

JEPHTHAH.

'T is well.   And can all be
removed?

HEZRON.

All can who live.

JEPHTHAH.

Then some are dead
and some
Must die? Who are they, Hezron, who?

HEZRON.

Even now
They pile the earth on Asher's noble
son,
And cover Menon's glorious face. Ke-
dar's
Life slowly ebbs away. The arrow
points,
The spears, have done their deadly work.
All else
Are doing well.

JEPHTHAH. *(Covering his face.)*

Alas! my friends: how dear
Were they to me. My counsellors are
gone.
I would they might have died in Miz-
peh. Oh!
'Tis hard to leave them here.

(He crosses the stage two or three times, then says:)

Our wounded ones—
Thou'lt see all is prepared to shield
from pain
And suffering by the way? Eber has
charge
Whene'er 'tis needful for their comfort-
ing,
To stay the band till they would fain
proceed.

HEZRON

Thou 'rt mindful, Jephthah, more than
　　is thy wont:
Thou 'st left these things to me before.

JEPHTHAH.

　　　　　　　　　　So now
I do, but I am sick of blood. Go now,
I trust thee, as I ever did. *(To Eber.)* To
　　rest:
A few short hours of calm repose will
　　fit
Us better for to-morrow's toil.

END OF SCENE SECOND.

Scene Third.

*Time, sunset.   A room opening upon a balcony facing
the west.   Telah and Adah alone.*

ADAH.

MOTHER, hast seen the sky more bright,
At golden sunset, than to-night?
See'st thou, how every quivering leaf
Stands out in delicate relief
Against the sky beyond, unrolled
Like some rich curtain's ample fold?
See, too, my gentle flowers, how they
Turn round to watch the close of day.
It seems as if, like me, they've power
T' enjoy the beauty of the hour.

There, softly creeping, Arnon's rills
Wind at the foot of Gilead's hills,
Twining, like silver threads, around
The base of each sun-lighted mound.
Dost thou not love to gaze, like me,
On all this gorgeous tracery,
As, gloriously, the weary sun
Sinks to his rest, when day is done?
In such an hour as this, would I,
Dear mother, lay me down to die;
Pillow my head, at close of day,
And pass, with sunset's light, away.

TELAH.

Surely it is a glorious sight,
And much I love its varied light,
Replete with fondest memory,
And thoughts of hope and love for
      thee;

But now my heart is far away.
Where is thy father, child, to-day?
A weight seems pressing on me here—
I hope the best, yet greatly fear
That in this conflict, some strong arm
May chance to do him serious harm.

ADAH.

Oh! mother, let such fears depart,
They're but a sickness of the heart,
Because he's gone so far from home:
Thou wilt be happier when he's
    come.
Jehovah's arm hath power, we know,
To shield from every deadly blow.
To Baalim, nor Ashtaroth, we
Have never learned to bow the knee,
And Israel's God, in whom we trust,
Is merciful, as well as just.

But why this new and fearful war
That calls my father off so far?
Why at the head of Gilead fight?
Surely, he 's not a Gileadite?

TELAH. (*As if communing with herself.*)

Yea, formerly he hath been one:—
Of Gilead, he 's the eldest son.

ADAH.

Then why dwell here, dear mother, say,
From his inheritance away?
Each Israelitish son hath space
Allotted for a dwelling-place,
And why should he forswear his home,
Within the wilderness to roam?
The desert land of Tob is not,
Like Canaan's soil, a favored spot.
And why did Gilead let him come?
His first-born son should dwell at home,

To cheer his sire's remaining space
Of life; then take his place.
Like foolish Esau, he hath not
His privilege so much forgot
That he should sell his birthright, and
Become a stranger in the land

TELAH.

He had no birthright.

ADAH.

                    And yet thou
Didst say, my mother, even now,
That he was Gilead's first-born son!

TELAH.

E'en so. What hath been done is done.
The wrongs thy father's youth befell,
Thy grandsire's shame, that I should
        tell.

It fitteth not, at least not now,
For on that fair and open brow
Thus early, it were sure to fling
Too much of sorrow's saddening;
Nor would I, with harsh memories,
Make lonelier such hours as these.

ADAH.

I 'll try to yield obedience,
But scarce can drive the feeling hence
To beg of thee to gratify,
This once, my curiosity;
For faint remembrances come o'er
Th' inquiring mind of scenes of yore:
Of hard-browed men that gathered
    round,
With voices threatening in their sound:
Of fleeing to the wilderness
To find us, there, a resting-place:—

Of other men, too, one by one,
Adding to Jephthah's strength their own,
Till, leader of a mighty clan,
They called him a most valiant man.
I've sometimes thought these things a
    dream—
For all such memories are dim—
But once, when in our garden-bower,
My father spent a lonely hour
Scanning the ground, with downcast
    eyes,
I thought to give a glad surprise,
So stole around, with noiseless step,
While on the ground his eyes he kept,
And communed with himself, as if
His heart was overcharged with grief.

TELAH.

But he said nothing, did he?

ADAH.

Yea.

TELAH.

Thou didst not listen?

ADAH.

Surely, nay,
At least, not meaningly; but I
Was there, thinking to catch his eye
Beaming with smiles, and hear him say
How is my little girl to-day?
So waiting, there I stood,—

TELAH.

And he
Talked with himself, and not with thee?
Thou should'st have come away.

ADAH.

I know
I ought, but did not then.

TELAH.

And so
Thou heard'st him talk—of what?

ADAH.

'T was of the past he spake: I thought
He called it dread and bitter past,
And wished Oblivion might cast
Her mantle over it, that he
Might all forget its memory:
That his was but an outcast's name,
Born to a heritage of shame;
Reproaches to endure from those
Who should be friends, but were his
    foes;
And that they yet should gladly claim
Kindred with Jephthah's hated name.
What more he said I did not hear,
For, trembling with an unknown fear,
    6

I turned away, marveling much
What dread calamity could touch
The secret springs that caused to flow
So bitterly those words of woe.
I wondered what dark heritage
Of shame could cloud his manly age;
If he had wronged his kinsmen, or
What else his heart was grieving for,
And yet no injury, I knew,
To friend or foe, could Jephthah do.
But who they were that yet should
  claim,
Gladly, connexion with his name,
I now can guess.

TELAH.

 How didst thou learn?

ADAH.

Theirs are the faces darkly stern,

Of those who, in my memory yet
Remain freshly as if I met
Them every day.   I do, at night,
Oft see them in my dreams,—the fright
Wakes me in terror, and I shroud
My face, and almost weep aloud.

TELAH.

I told thee naught.

ADAH.

                    Save thou didst say
That *he* was Gilead's son; and they
Are his younger brethren.   Is't not so?

TELAH.

Thou hast conjectured right—and know
The time, of which he spake, is come:
Entreatingly called home, by those
Thou heard'st him mention as his foes,

He, even now, their leader, fights
Against th' encroaching Ammonites.

ADAH.

Mother, thy words encourage me;
Wilt thou not tell me who was she
That gave him birth?

TELAH.

                    She was no Jew
Of Jacob's line, but lineage drew
From outcast Ishmael.   The sire
Of thine saw her and loved.   Desire
Sprung up—no law had made them one,
And yet the fruit—

ADAH.

          Was what?

TELAH.

                    A son.

ADAH.

Long, long have I conjectured this,
That some such sad remembrances
Clouded my father's cheerless past,
And darkness, o'er his future cast;
Yet scarcely deemed such mark of shame
Was stamped upon my father's name;
That God's own courts, to enter in,
He could not, so defiled with sin.
Ere this such truth I should have heard:
Innocently I may have erred,
But then thou knowest, and canst tell,
If thou hast conned this matter well.

TELAH.

To none, my child, has wrong been
    done,
And, least of all, to Eslon's son.
God, in his mercy, gave to us

No sons to feel this dreaded curse,
But one dear child, whose progeny
From all such stain is counted free.

ADAH.

Then will I grieve o'er it no more,
The past no sorrow can restore.
But what of her—dear mother, say,
Hath yet the earth-worm claimed its
 prey?
Far better fate than it would be
To lead such life of misery.

TELAH.

She was forsaken soon and spurned
By him whose flattering tongue had
 learned
Her heart to throb with feelings wild
For one whose passion had beguiled

Her into sin.   She sought return
To her own country, there to mourn,
Till death should come, the final loss
Of that to which all else is dross.
Nor long did she her frailty weep,
And tearful vigils nightly keep,
But like those clouds, at close of day,
Gently and calmly passed away.
O'er her cold corse fresh flowers they
    strewed,
And, with their tears, her grave bedewed,
For she was fair and beautiful
As roses that we love to cull,
And like a bud, with canker worn,
Or from its stem that's rudely torn,
She faded in her loveliness,
Yet lives in *their* remembrances
Who knew her ere her heart was crushed,
And its sweet music sadly hushed.

ADAH.

And then my grandsire took a wife?

TELAH.

He did before; and bitter strife
Was mingled with each household
        word,
While angry thoughts and feelings
        stirred
The breasts of those *she* bare to him,
And, with success, they strove to dim
A father's love for his first-born,
That they, with words of biting scorn,
Might cast him out. The deed was done,
The father sanctioned, and the son
Warned to depart, while tauntingly
They jeered him with fierce mockery;
Scoffed at his birth, saying "The son
Of a strange woman should be gone:"

Nay, more; with brutal violence
They *thrust* him out, and *drove* him
    thence.

*   *   *   *   *   *   *

Aye! there are words that tear apart
The fibers of the crushing heart;
That stretch its fragile strings so much
They burst asunder, at a touch;
That sweep its gentle chords of song
With floods of grief so wild and
    strong,
That harsh, discordant sounds alone
Swell forth, in place of happier tone;
Yea, that, with master-passion fraught,
Drive out each sweet and peaceful
    thought,
Till perish all the flowers of feeling,
Its naked depths alone revealing.

ADAH.

Mother, they're past, those dreary years
Of insult, wrong, and burning tears,
And now the wronged one, with his calm
And quiet dignity, like the palm,
Judea's stately emblem, soon will be
Ruler of Gilead, for victory
Shall crown his efforts, and all they
Who mocked at him shall feel his sway;
His mild and gentle yet decided rule
That bows the trusting heart and leaves
    it full
Of meek submission, timid love and awe,
To find his slightest wish, his look, a
    law.
How my glad thoughts go springing forth
    to meet
My precious sire, whose every wish 't is
    sweet

For me, at all times, gladly to obey.
Mother, how lonely 'tis, when he's away;
The house is desolate, the dusky walls
Sad echoes whisper, as my footstep falls
Lightly upon the stone-paved courts
  and I
Hear solemn wailings in each night-bird's
  cry.
The bulbul, 'mid the clumps of roses,
  where
The fountain throws its spray upon the air,
Weeps mournful plaining at the midnight
  hour
From out the fragrance of her fav'rite
  bower,
And my sad heart seems shrouded with
  its own
Dismal forebodings, when we're thus
  alone.

TELAH.

Cheer thee, my child—patiently hope
  the best,
The hour is drawing nigh for nightly
  rest.
Thou 'rt weary and dispirited, sweet
  child,
And the dark tale, I told thee, hath
  beguiled
No one of those dark shadows from a
  brow
Where they 've too often cast their gloom,
  ere now.
Throw them aside, and that thy happy
  dreams
May be as sunlight on the flashing streams
Of fair Judea's soil, thy lute bring here,
And pour its melody within my ear,
To charm *my* boding heart of all *its* fear.

ADAH.

Wilt listen, mother, while I sing?

TELAH.

Ah, yes,
For ever had thy voice a power to
bless
From the first hour its feeble wail was
heard,
And all a mother's love my bosom
stirred,
Up to this night of painful solitude,
When dark'ning shadows drape the fad-
ing wood,
And settle gloomily upon my soul.
Yea, sing; music may yet control
The fiercely struggling powers as I shall
hear
Thy pleasant melodies fall on my ear.

(Adah claps her hands and a young girl enters.)

ADAH.

Miriam, bring hither now thy lute and
    play
Thy choicest melodies, to drive our gloom
    away.
Meanwhile, to thy accompanying, I'll
    sing.

*(Miriam retires for a moment, and, returning, begins
a prelude on her instrument.   Adah sings, Miriam
accompanying.)*

ADAH AND MIRIAM.

SONG.

O! why should hearts be sad
When there's so much to glad?
When earth, so bright and fair,
Should charm our every care?

Judea's vales are green,
Judea's skies, serene,
Judea's maidens, fair,
Her sons brave, every-where.

CHORUS.

Then let our hearts, to-night,
Beat high, with pulses light,
And glad the fleeting hours
With music, joy, and flowers.

SONG.

Judea's sons will toil
For honor's goodly spoil,
And with the bold and free
Wait glorious destiny.
Judea's maidens, fair,
Sustain, with loving care,
Daughter, sister, and wife,
The crowning gift of life.

CHORUS.

Then let our hearts, to-night,
Beat high, with pulses light,
And glad the fleeting hours
With music, love, and flowers.

ADAH.

Sadly my voice seemeth to jar
  With all such bright imagining;
I turn to him, who still afar,
  I'd fain to this lone circle bring

SONG.

Night draweth on and we're alone
  Within a stranger land,
We long to see and cling to thee,
  Grasping thy friendly hand;
            Father, come home.

The sighing breeze sweeps thro' the
    trees
  With such a dreary sound,
I turn my head to list thy tread:
  Thou art not to be found;
        Father, come home.

The sun's last ray, athwart the way,
  Lengthens the plane-tree's shade,
While evening's gloom steals thro' the
    room,
  And darkness fills the glade;
        Father, come home.

The tinkling bells, adown the dells,
  Where browsing camels stray,
With drowsy chime, recall the time,
  When thou wert not away;
        Father, come home.

7

Sad are our hearts when day departs,
  And twinkling stars appear,
With milder light, to rule the night,
  Whispering thou art not here;
          Father, come home.

*(An attendant enters, and, with a low obeisance,
  hands a missive to Telah. She clips the thread and
  reads aloud.)*

"Rejoice with me, my loved ones there,
The strife is ended.   I prepare
E'en now to take my homeward way,
Victor in this most mighty fray.
Aroer, Minnith, twenty cities yield
To Gilead on the bloody field.
His arm gave strength, our foes to over-
      come,
Those Ammonites, and now for joy and
      home!"

TELAH.

Miriam, it is the hour for evening service,
    call
Our minstrels to come hither, one and
    all,
To join together in a glorious song
For all Jehovah's done. To him be-
    long
Deep gratitude for what *His* hand hath
    wrought;
That through a land with danger thickly
    fraught
He hath preserved the husband, father,
    friend,
And master: praise to Jehovah without
    end.

*(Miriam retires to execute Telah's commands, and
    Idah resumes her singing.)*

ADAH.

His hand kept thee, unscathed and free,
Through all war's wild alarm,
And we 'll rejoice, with heart and voice,
To greet thee, free from harm;
Father, come home.

*(Musicians enter and arrange themselves, and Telah
addresses them.)*

TELAH. *(To the musicians.)*

Your boldest, gladdest strains to-night
will be   [and me,
The most approved by this young maid
Jephthah, unharmed, in a few days will
come
To greet us all within our quiet home,
For signal victory his arms hath crowned,
And Gilead gains the wide-spread
country round;

And now, proud Israel's ruler, he,
From such a conquest, is most sure to be.

SONG.

On they came with power and might,
Like a torrent of the night,
And they struggled in the fight,
But Jehovah's mighty hand
Scattered the presumptuous band,
And *He* drove them from the land.

One voice chanting.—Trust in Jehovah, for *He* is mighty, and His mercy endureth forever.

All the efforts made, must fail
Of the gods, that rule the vale
Chemosh, Ashtaroth and Baal.
Of Jehovah's power we tell
With the victories that befell
Wandering, chosen Israel.

Voice chanting.—Trust in Jehovah, &c.

Earth must yield her to *His* nod,
Princes bow and kiss *His* rod,
Heathen nations own *Him* God,
Mighty, merciful and just,
Hurling nations to the dust
When they cease in *Him* to trust

Voice chanting.—Trust in Jehovah, &c.

Yet the lowliest ever may
Feel His mighty arm their stay,
As they travel on their way;
So, to no vain idol cling,
But the heart's pure offering
To Jehovah-jireth bring.

Voice chanting.—Trust in Jehovah, for
He is mighty, and His mercy endureth
forever.

END OF SCENE THIRD.

Scene Fourth.

Jephthah, a few followers with him, approaching his home in Mizpeh. He dismisses them.

JEPHTHAH.

Go, now, my tried and trusty followers,
And as each one shall take his homeward
way,
May ye, arrived, in mercy find 't is well
With those ye left behind. E'en so, with
me,
That I find, too, all's well within the
walls
That hold my heart's most precious ones.
Farewell.

*(They disappear in different directions, and he
soliloquizes.)*

Why sinks my heart with such chill
    weight of dread?
Why shake my knees, as if no strength
    were left
In this strong, stalwart frame, as I do
    look
Upon the sheltering boughs above the
    roof
Where dwell my treasures all?   My eyes
    are dim;
They have no power to look at those
    gray walls
That pen my little fold—the youngling
    and
Its dam.—Home! sweetest spot of all
    the earth.
A few more eager steps, and I am there;

Yet something still those longing steps
   restrains.
What if she haste to meet me here?—
   or that
Dear one, my other self?   Oh! would
   't were past
That I might know the worst, and know-
   ing, fear
No more.   Uncertainty! how dread the
   thought
Of what this hand may be compelled
   to do.

*(Music is heard, and Adah comes with tabrets and
   dances to meet him.)*

'T is she! 't is she!   My one ewe lamb!
   Oh, this
Is more than I can bear!   Most duti-
   ful
And loving child of all Judea's maids,

She comes, with signs of overmastering
    joy,
To greet her sire, who dooms his child
    to death
In all her virgin innocence! Punished!
And more, for all my wild ambition
    now.

*(Adah, seeing his wild, disordered looks and torn
garments, stops.)*

ADAH.

O! Father, speak to me.

*(Jephthah, having covered his face with his hands,
as if to shut her from his sight, stands motion-
less.)*

          He will not speak,
He will not look at me!

JEPHTHAH.

            I can not, for
My heart is burst with grief.

Jephthah's Return.

ADAH.

Who speaks of grief,
Returning from such signal victory?
Leader of Gilead—

JEPHTHAH.

O! name it not—
Most hateful thought that ever crossed
my brain.

ADAH.

Greatly rejoiced my mother dear and I
To hear the tidings of thy messenger,
And scarce have slept for very joy, that
thou
Wast safe from all the dangers that beset
Thy path among such deadly foes.
Thou com'st,
And with a daughter's loving tenderness

And overflowing sympathy, with what
I deemed thy great, full joy at this that
    shall
Exalt thee over Gilead, I haste
To meet thee with a gladdened step.
    Not one
Embrace! no father's fond, warm kiss!
    nor one
Sweet word of loving welcome! O! not
    e'en
A look! O! father, what means this?
    When thou
Hast come from off the hills with all
    thine armed
Men proudly at thy back, with valor
    flushed,
Thou'st bade me to thy arms, as if
    't were joy
Beyond the battle's victory, to clasp

Thy child again.   But now, thou heed'st
  me not!.

JEPHTHAH.

My daughter, thou hast brought me very
  low.

ADAH.

I, father!

JEPHTHAH.

Thou 'rt one of them that trouble me.

ADAH.

What have I done?   Thou dost not hate
  me now?
It can not be!   Thou lov'st me, father?
  Say
But that, and I can bear it all!

JEPHTHAH.

Love thee,

My precious child!—yea, better than
my life.

ADAH.

I knew 't was so, yet thou didst look so
cold;

Had no kind word of greeting for mine
ear—

I have done naught to anger thee?

JEPHTHAH.

Nay, nay—

Thou never didst, my own sweet child.
Thou gav'st

Me never slightest cause for grief, till now.

ADAH.

Why now?   Pray tell me all.   Strong
' in thy love,

And in the sweet assurance of such
    cheering words,
I 'm ready for the worst.   Fear not for
    me.
'T were better over.   Let the pang, I
    pray, be short.

JEPHTHAH.

I 've opened to the Lord my mouth; I
    can
Not now go back——

ADAH.

My father, if unto the Lord, thy God,
Thou 'st opened thy mouth, do unto me
According to the vow thy lips have made,
For on our enemies, the Ammonites,
His vengeance hath he taken by thy
    hand.

JEPHTHAH.

My child, thou break'st my heart!

ADAH.

Nay, father, nay—
My disobedience and disregard
Of all Jehovah's laws *would* break thy
    heart.
Do I not owe to thee my life?   And
    should
That life be dearer to me than the
    right?
Than Jephthah's full approval of his
    God?
I 'm Jephthah's child, his only one, and
    should
Men say in Israel: "She did defy
The law, mocked at her father's words;
    set them

At naught?" That were far worse than
    death, for God,
Thy God, hath armed thy right hand
    with *His* power;—
Hath smote thine enemies before thy
    face,
E'en as thou asked. And now, shall we
    withhold
That which thy lips did promise unto
    Him?
We *dare* not mock Him thus: a jealous
    God
He is, and the iniquity of him
That doeth wrong shall be (thou know'st
    the law)
Upon his children surely visited.
I could not then escape. 'T is not so
    great
A sacrifice.

8

JEPHTHAH.

O! say not so!   My all,
And nothing else.   O, reckless vow!
    O, wild
Ambition to be first, where I have been
Spurned and insulted!   Mad desire to
    show
Jehovah's power in me; that *He* ap-
    proved
The banished brother, unacknowledged
    son!
Pride! pride! the great archangel's
    damning sin,
That drove him out of Paradise!   Ah,
    me!
My punishment, like Cain's, is more
    than I
Can bear.   He slew his brother, only; I
Must kill my child.

ADAH.

Not thus did Job bewail
His children slain, his wealth all rifled
    in
An hour.   Not thus did faithful Abra-
    ham,
When God, to try his faith, commanded
    him /
To take his only son, the promised seed,
To lone Moriah's steep, and offer him
Upon its heights, a smoking sacrifice.
Yea, father, in Jehovah, God, trust now
As thou hast ever done: He doeth right.

JEPHTHAH.

I thank thee for those words.   'T is the
    one drop
That 's pleasant in this cup of bitterness,
That hopeful thought of holy Abraham.

God did provide the lamb: He may
again.

ADAH.

Nay, nay, I meant not that—only that
he
Did not bewail or hesitate, when God
Commanded him to take his only son,
The promised seed, in whom all nations
should
Be blessed, and bind him to the ready
pile.
I had forgot the rest.

JEPHTHAH.

And so should I.
Daughter, I am rebuked. God did but
try
His faith. I must be punished for my
sin,

For that desire of exaltation, so intense
That it forgot all else.

*(Adah makes no reply, but stands with one hand over
her eyes, her head bent down in a thoughtful atti-
tude. Jephthah noticing it, and seeing she makes
no reply to what he has said, gloomily continues,
as if to himself.)*

I wonder not she has no word for me.

ADAH.

I have; I have.   What askest thou?
    My mind
Was buried in its thoughts.

JEPHTHAH.

            And I would ask
What were those thoughts?

ADAH.

        Of death, of leaving thee,
My mother, all I love; to be no more.

Of the dark grave, and what a contrast
  in
My early youth to lay me down within
Its narrow walls, shut from the glorious
  light
Of heaven; and for companionship,
  instead
Of thee and her, the greedy, gloating
  worm.

JEPHTHAH, *(weeping.)*

Go on.

ADAH.

The shivering cold for warmth, darkness
For light, silence for pleasant sounds,
  these limbs,
Rigid and still, instead of airy life's
Quick, varied movements; and drear
  loneliness

For most beloved companionship. Yet think

Not that I shrink, appalling though it be—

Right must be done, whate'er the cost to me.

I have no fear; like Job, I, too, can say,

"Though worms devour this skin of mine, yet in

My flesh shall I see God." Father, thy vow

Must be fulfilled! Yet make I one request.

JEPHTHAH.

Thou couldst ask nothing that I would not grant.

ADAH.

Give me, I pray thee, two short months, in which

I may prepare me for my fate.   Thou
    know'st
What was to be.   I did look forward to
The time, my height of joy should be
    to make
Another happy, and I thought too
    much,
It may be, of the bliss that should be
    mine
When yet another should dwell in our
    home,
Alike beloved by *her* and *thee* and me,
And sons and daughters should be born
    to thee
In place of those Jehovah had denied
To thine own wedlock.   No sweet,
    cherub lip,
Pressed close to mine, shall ever call
    me by

That dearest name that woman ever
    bore.
I 'll not repine; my grief is not my own:
'T is *thine*, and *hers*, and his. O, God!
    for *him*—

JEPHTHAH.

My daughter, Adah, wilt thou break
    my heart?

ADAH.

Nay, father, nay; but I do think of
    him,—
Eber, in all his young and joyous years
Doomed to be desolate; to bear a heart
Widowed, bereaved, just as he enters on
Life's opening threshhold; his bright
    morning sky
Beclouded ere life's sun had fairly risen.

Thou wilt console him; let him be to
  thee
E'en as he would have been, although
  no bride
His yearning heart find here.   Thou 'lt
  promise this?

JEPHTHAH.

I promise all.   Say on.   Ask what thou
  wilt.

ADAH.

My mother loves me, father.   O! how
  can
She bear to be alone?   Her child reft
  from
Her arms, and none to dwell with her:
  alone!
Oh! comfort her.

JEPHTHAH.

And who shall comfort me?
Thou think'st of all, of every one but
    me.
Hast thou no love for me?   Shall *I* not,
    too,
Be left alone?   Will not *my* home be
    dark?—
My heart be desolate?   Hast thou no
    love
For *me*, my child?

ADAH.

Ah, yes, too much for all.
Forgive me if I thought of others first,
Each is so dear; it is so hard to feel
I can no longer have a place among
Ye all; can come no more with heart
    so full

Of gushing love, to cheer in sorrow,
   soothe
In suffering hours, and be a part of all,
In joy or grief.

JEPHTHAH.

    Look, Adah; there she comes!
How shall I meet her? Oh! how break
To her this woe?

ADAH.

    I will away, I can
Not meet her now. Thy blessing, once
   more,
Father, on thine Adah's head.

*(She kneels. He places his hand on her head. Telah
comes in full view, as he does it, and the curtain
drops.)*

END OF SCENE FOURTH.

Mourning over the Grave.

Scene Fifth.

"And the daughters of Israel went out, four days in the year, to mourn and lament for her."

Scene—the mountain, with trees and rocks. A green mound, under which are the remains of Jephthah's daughter. To one side, and partially hidden, is Eber, the betrothed of Adah, bowed under a covering of sackcloth. From the opposite side of the stage advance six maidens, clad in white robes, carrying baskets of flowers, and singing as they come.

MAIDENS.

SONG.

Here we come, a band of maidens,
   To these lonely rocks and glades;
Bright the blue sky bends above us,
   Cool and green, the leafy shades.

Come we here to mourn a lost one,
   Loved and lost one to bewail:
Fitting spot for lamentation
   O'er our lost one of the vale.

It was here she was lamenting,
   Till two moons had paled and gone,
Gaining strength, and faith, and courage,
   In these solitudes, alone.

On the mountain, where she perished,
   Where she spent those lonely days,
Every year we come to mourn her,
   Come, this noble maid to praise.

*(They discover Eber sitting on the far side of the
mound. He slowly raises the sackcloth from his
face, and they see who it is. A maiden speaks.)*

MAIDEN.

Comest thou here to mourn and weep,
Eber? Worthy was she that's here
Beneath this lonely mound.

EBER.

Ye come
But once a year, for she was naught
To you but a sweet friend.   To me
My sun, my life—my every thing;
And I come—when, I scarcely know,
Nor, yet, how long I stay.   There is
No joy remaining, now, save here
To bow by this green mound and
    feel
I shall be with her soon.   How long!
How long! Oh, cruel vow! Was
    He,
The God of mercy, pleased with such
A sacrifice?

MAIDEN

Eber, thou griev'st
As one that hath no hope.

EBER.

Grief is
No name for all the pangs I feel;
For, with such love as I have borne,
'T is the survivor dies.   Long woe,
With ecstasy of torture, kills
At last—but O! how long.   No death
The dying hath, like unto that
The living feels, to wander on
Alone; of all earth's joys bereft—
Its glorious sun extinct; life's light
To darkness turned, and all its flowers
To noxious weeds; the poor, numb soul,
Unknowing when 't is change of day,
Or night, or seasons, e'en.   The crushed,
Torn heart-strings, rent away from all
About which twined their joy,
Lie trampled, bleeding, thrilled with
    pain,

And yet there's no desire to take
Them up, and soothe, and nurse them
    back
To ease, and strength, and life again.
The once glad, joyous heart, bound-
    ing
In youthful gladsomeness, crushed down,
A heavy lead-like thing within
The bosom's core, which ne'er again
Uplifts itself, but slowly wears
Its lingering tenement away,
Mourning a form that hath none,
    and
A voice it can not hear.

(He slowly moves away.)

(Six voices chanting separately, as numbered.)

FIRST VOICE.

Joy beamed in her eye as she went forth
    to meet him.

9

SECOND VOICE.

Skill born of her gladness brought mirth
from the tabret.

THIRD VOICE.

Fleet moved her light steps in the joy
of his coming.

FOURTH VOICE.

She met him; her eye beamed no longer
in brightness.

FIFTH VOICE.

Dropped quickly her fingers, forgetting
their cunning.

SIXTH VOICE.

And stayed were the steps that had
bounded in gladness.

FIRST VOICE.

But paled not the cheek of the maid as
she listened.

SECOND VOICE.

Her people were saved—she was ready
to perish.

THIRD VOICE.

Meek, bent the young head in its quiet
submission.

FOURTH VOICE.

O! daughter of Jephthah, most worthy
of honor.

FIFTH VOICE.

Nor daughter of Jephthah alone, but
of Israel.

SIXTH VOICE.

A nation laments while its maids are
bewailing.

ALL.

And the tribes of the earth, through all
time, shall thee honor.

SONG.

Daughter, in thy narrow bed,
Sister, from whom life hath fled,
Jewish maiden, o'er thy head,
Loving hands delight to fling
Sweetest blossoms of the spring
Nature's holy offering.

*(They scatter flowers upon the mound from their
    baskets, and continue to do it, from time to time,
    through the song.)*

Jewish maiden, virtues rare
Made thee e'en more good, than fair;
Pure as ever maidens are;
Meekly bent her drooping head,
Every thought of self had fled—
"Father, be 't as thou hast said.'

Other daughters have been good,
But, among them, she hath stood
Crown of virgin womanhood.

Round this mound sad hearts await,
Here to weep thine early fate,
And thy goodness emulate.

Jewish maiden! fair and young,
Ever shall thy praise be sung,
All the maids of earth among.
Purity beamed in thine eye—
All the virtues that could die
Wafted thy pure soul on high.

(Six voices chanting, each a separate sentiment.)

FIRST VOICE.

Whose heart was so strong as this beautiful maid's?

SECOND VOICE.

Whose filial devotion so perfect and pure?

THIRD VOICE.

No son of Judea was like unto her.

FOURTH VOICE.

Who'll teach us our duty now she lieth
low?

FIFTH VOICE.

The maidens of Israel are poor in her
loss.

SIXTH VOICE.

The God of our fathers make us, even
us,

ALL.

Like unto the maiden we come to
bewail.

SONG.

Woe! for the vow that the warrior made,
The warrior and father, that Ammon be
stayed,
And his country be freed from the grasp
of the foe,

Who the altars of God in the valleys
 laid low.

Bereaved is a household—*one* heart is a
 wreck,
Which thought for the bridal, its treasure
 to deck;
Her life is aweary, uncheered, and
 alone,
There beameth no future when hope is
 unknown.

Sleep sweetly, pure maiden, disturbed
 by no fears,
We'll keep the turf green by our sorrowing tears,
And the blossoms we bring thee, renew
 when they fade,
Lamenting, bewailing thee, beautiful
 maid.

SONG.

(With voices alternating.)

ONE VOICE.

He that sleeps, shall wake no more.

ALL.

Yes, upon the morrow.

ONE VOICE.

Years, the dead can not restore.

ALL.

But they ease our sorrow.

ONE VOICE.

All must die, though live they would—

ALL.

Every life's a debtor.

ONE VOICE.

Weeping, mourning, do no good,—

ALL.

Sadness maketh better.

ONE VOICE.

It is sad to mourn and weep.

ALL.

Sad, and yet a pleasure.

ONE VOICE.

Let each sorrowing memory sleep.

ALL.

Memory is a treasure.
Memories of the pure and good
 Make our own hearts better.
This pure maiden, if we could,
 We would not forget her.

SONG.

They met, and proud Ammon was conquered at last,
And the tramp of his warriors went
 hurrying past;

His towns and his cities were swept from
  his hands,
And the conquered oppressor hath sought
  other lands.

There's a chieftain in Israel, once haughty
  and bold,
But the light, in his dark eye, is altered
  and cold;
There's a Judge, too, in Israel, loves justice and right,
But the honors, they pay him, can bring
  no delight.

He knoweth the price of proud Ammon's
  defeat,
For a face is upturning, so pleadingly
  sweet;
'T is the picture that's ever his vision
  before,

And 't will fade from his sight, nevermore, nevermore.

There's a memory, haunting, will never
   depart,
And the sweet light of hope is shut out
   of his heart.
He is ruler, he's judge, but he's child-
   less and lone,
For *her* life was the price of the victories
   won.

SONG.

(With alternate voices, one alone, and all answering.)

ONE VOICE.

Sing of all that's good and fair,

ALL.

She was better fairer:

ONE VOICE.

Sing of all that's bright and rare,

ALL.

She was brighter, rarer.

ONE VOICE.

Liken her to earth's flower-queen,

ALL.

Lily of the valley.

ONE VOICE.

Breathing fragrance, though unseen

ALL.

When the light winds dally

ONE VOICE.

Liken her to brighter flowers,

ALL.

Sharon's precious roses,

ONE VOICE.

Making glad the passing hours

ALL.

As each cup uncloses.

ONE VOICE.

Liken her to stars of night;

ALL.

They're too far above us;

ONE VOICE.

They are pure, and they are bright,

ALL.

But they can not love us.

ONE VOICE.

Liken her to all pure things;

ALL.

Snow upon the mountain;
Dewdrops,   snow,   and   flowers   and
        springs;
Water from the fountain.

Yet is naught so pure and bright,
    As this peerless daughter,
Turning meekly from the light
    To the dark doom brought her.

CLOSING SONG.

(One Voice.)

Her life bought our freedom,
 For the nation paid;
Israel can but honor
 This devoted maid.

Prophet's hymning, tender,
 Ready writer's praise,
Ever shall commend her,
 Through all lapse of days.

And though Israel perish,
 Prophet, priest, and king,
Yet the world shall cherish
 Her of whom we sing.

Distant times and sages
 Shall her fame rehearse,
Ages upon ages
 Weave it into verse.

And no brighter luster
   Ever deed surround,
Never mem'ry juster,
   Through all time be found.

All the world shall claim her,
   Like the sun and showers,
Though we love to name her
   Israel's and ours.

END OF SCENE FIFTH.

www.ingramcontent.com/pod-product-compliance
Lightning Source LLC
Chambersburg PA
CBHW030904050726
47500CB00009B/1008